THE CONSTITUTION OF THE UNITED STATES OF AMERICA

The Bill of Rights & All Amendments

BY THE CONSTITUTION OF
THE UNITED STATES OF AMERICA

Contents

THE UNITED STATES CONSTITUTION   1

  (Preamble)   1

  Article I - The Legislative   1

    Section 1 – Congress   1

    Section 2 - The House of Representatives   2
      Clause 1 - Congressional Districting
      Clause 2 - Qualification of Members of Congress
      Clause 3 - Apportionment of Seats in the House
      Clause 4 - Vacancies
      Clause 5 - Officers and Power of Impeachment

    Section 3 - The Senate   3
      Clause 1 - Composition and Selection
      Clause 2 - Classes of Senators
      Clause 3 - Qualifications
      Clause 4 - The Vice President
      Clause 5 - Officers
      Clause 6 - Trial of Impeachment
      Clause 7 - Judgments on Impeachment

    Section 4 – Elections   4
      Clause 1 - Congressional Power to Regulate
      Clause 2 - Time of Assembling

    Section 5 - Powers and Duties of the House   4
      Clause 1 - Power to Judge Elections
      Clause 2 - Rules of Proceedings
      Clause 3 - Duty to Keep a Journal
      Clause 4 - Adjournments

    Section 6 - Rights and Disabilities of Members   5

    Clause 1 - Compensation and Immunities
    Clause 2 - Disabilities

Section 7 - Legislative Process   6
    Clause 1 - Revenue Bills
    Clause 2 - Approval by the President
    Clause 3 - Presentation of Resolutions

Section 8 - Powers of Congress   7
    Clause 1 - Power to Tax and Spend
    Clause 2 - Borrowing Power
    Clause 3- Commerce Power
    Clause 4 - Naturalization and Bankruptcies
    Clause 5 - Money
    Clause 6 - Money
    Clause 7 - Post Office
    Clause 8 - Copyrights and Patent
    Clause 9- Creating of Courts
    Clause 10 - Maritime Crimes
    Clause 11 - War; Military Establishment
    Clause 12 - War; Military Establishment
    Clause 13 - War; Military Establishment
    Clause 14 - War; Military Establishment
    Clause 15 - The Militia
    Clause 16 - The Militia
    Clause 17 - District of Columbia; Federal Property
    Clause 18 - Necessary Clause

Section 9 - Powers Denied Congress   9
    Clause 1 - Importation of Slaves
    Clause 2 - *Habeas Corpus* Suspension
    Clause 3 - Bill of Attainder and *Ex Post Facto* Laws
    Clause 4 - Taxes
    Clause 5 - Duties on Exports from States
    Clause 6- Preference to Ports
    Clause 7- Appropriations and Accounting of Public Money
    Clause 8 - Titles of Nobility; Presents

Section 10 - Powers Denied to the States 10
    Clause 1 - Not to Make Treaties, Coin Money, Pass *Ex Post Facto* Laws, Impair Contracts
    Clause 2 - Not to Levy Duties on Exports and Imports
    Clause 3 - Not to Lay Tonnage Duties, Keep Troops, Make Compacts, or Engage in War

Article II – Executive 10

  Section 1 - The President 10
    Clause 1 - Powers and Term of the President
    Clause 2 - Election
    Clause 3 - Election
    Clause 4 - Election
    Clause 5 - Qualifications
    Clause 6 - Presidential Succession
    Clause 7 - Compensation and Emolument
    Clause 8 - Oath of Office

  Section 2 - Powers and Duties of the President 13
    Clause 1 - Commander-in-Chiefship; Presidential Advisers;
    Clause 2 - Treaties and Appointment of Officers
    Clause 3 - Vacancies during Recess of Senate

  Section 3 - Legislative, Diplomatic, and Law Enforcement 13

  Section 4 – Impeachment 14

Article III – Judicial 14

  Section 1 - Judicial Power, Courts, Judges 14

  Section 2 - Judicial Power and Jurisdiction 14
    Clause 1 - Cases and Controversies; Grants of Jurisdiction
    Clause 2 - Original and Appellate Jurisdiction; Exceptions and Regulations of Appellate Jurisdiction
    Clause 3 - Trial by Jury

  Section 3 – Treason 15
    Clause 1 - Definition and Limitations
    Clause 2 - Punishment

Article IV - States' Relations ... 16
    Section 1 - Full Faith and Credit ... 16
    Section 2 - Interstate Comity ... 16
        Clause 1 - State Citizenship: Privileges and Immunities
        Clause 2 - Interstate Rendition
        Clause 3 - Fugitives from Labor
    Section 3 - Admission of New States to Union; Property of United State ... 16
        Clause 1 - Admission of New States to Union
        Clause 2 - Property of the United States
    Section 4 - Obligations of United States to States ... 17

Article V - Mode of Amendment ... 17

Article VI - Prior Debts, National Supremacy, Oaths of Office ... 18
    Clause 1 - Validity of Prior Debts and Engagements
    Clause 2 - Supremacy of the Constitution, Laws and Treaties
    Clause 3 - Oath of Office

Article VII – Ratification ... 18

Letter of Transmittal ... 23

Letter of Transmittal to the President of Congress ... 25
Amendments to the Constitution ... 27
    (The Preamble to The Bill of Rights) ... 27
    (Articles I through X are known as the Bill of Rights)
        Article [I] - Freedom of expression and religion ... 28
        Article [II] - Bearing Arms ... 29
        Article [III] - Quartering Soldiers ... 29
        Article [IV] - Search and Seizure ... 29
        Article [V] - Rights of Persons ... 29

Article [VI] - Rights of Accused in Criminal Prosecutions	30
Article [VII] - Civil Trials	30
Article [VIII] - Further Guarantees in Criminal Cases	30
Article [IX] - Unenumerated Rights	30
Article [X] - Reserved Powers	31

[Article XI] - Suits Against States 31

[Article XII] - Election of President 31

Article XIII - Slavery and Involuntary Servitude 33

    Section 1 - Slavery and Involuntary Servitude

    Section 2 - Enforcement

Article XIV - Rights Guaranteed: Privileges and Immunities of Citizenship, Due Process, and Equal Protection 33

    Section 1 - Rights Guaranteed

    Section 2 - Apportionment of Representation

    Section 3 - Disqualification and Public Debt

    Section 4 - Disqualification and Public Debt

    Section 5 - Enforcement

Article XV - Rights of Citizens to Vote 34

Article XVI - Income Tax 35

[Article XVII] - Popular Election of Senators 35

    Section 1

    Section 2

    Section 3

Article [XVIII] - Prohibition of Intoxicating Liquor 36

    Section 1 - Prohibition of Intoxicating Liquors

Section 2 - Congress and the several States shall have concurrent power

Section 3 - Ratification

Article [XIX] - Women's Suffrage Rights ... 36

Section 1 - Women's Suffrage Rights

Section 2 - Enforcement

Article [XX] - Terms of President, Vice President, Members of Congress: Presidential Vacancy ... 36

Section 1 - Terms of President, Vice President, Senators, and Representatives

Section 2 - Time of assembling Congress

Section 3 - Filling vacancy in office of President

Section 4 - Power of Congress in Presidential succession

Section 5 - Time of taking effect

Section 6 - Ratification

Article [XXI] - Repeal of Eighteenth Amendment ... 38

Section 1 - Repeal of Eighteenth Amendment

Section 2 - Transportation of intoxicating liquors

Section 3 - Ratification

Amendment XXII - Presidential Tenure ... 38

Section 1 - Presidential Tenure

Section 2 - Enforcement

Amendment XXIII - Presidential Electors for the District of Columbia ... 39

Section 1 - Presidential Electors for the District of Columbia

Section 2 - Enforcement

Amendment XXIV - Abolition of the Poll Tax
Qualification in Federal Elections   39

Amendment XXV - Presidential Vacancy,
Disability, and Inability   40

Amendment XXVI - Reduction of Voting Age Qualification   41

    Section 1 - Reduction of Voting Age Qualification

    Section 2 - Enforcement

Amendment XXVII - Congressional Pay Limitation   41

NOTES   43

Dates - Milestone dates for the constitution,
bill of rights and the start of the U.S. government.   45

Spellings   47
Vocabulary   49
Subject Index   57
Ratifications   67

    Jun 21, 1788 Constitution   67

    Dec 15, 1791 (Articles I through X are
    known as the Bill of Rights)   70

        Article [I] - Freedom of expression and religion

        Article [II] - Bearing Arms

        Article [III] - Quartering Soldiers

        Article [IV] - Search and Seizure

        Article [V] - Rights of Persons

        Article [VI] - Rights of Accused in Criminal Prosecutions

        Article [VII] - Civil Trials

        Article [VIII] - Further Guarantees in Criminal Cases

        Article [IX] - Unenumerated Rights

        Article [X] - Reserved Powers

Feb 7, 1795 [Article XI] - Suits Against States	70
Jun 15, 1804 [Article XII] - Election of President	71
Dec 6, 1865 Article XIII - Slavery and Involuntary Servitude	72
Jul 9, 1868 Article XIV - Rights Guaranteed: Privileges and Immunities of Citizenship, Due Process, and Equal Protection	73
Feb 3, 1870 Article XV - Rights of Citizens to Vote	74
Feb 3, 1913 Article XVI - Income Tax	75
Apr 8, 1913 [Article XVII] - Popular Election of Senators	76
Jan 16, 1919 Article [XVIII] - Prohibition of Intoxicating Liquors	77
Aug 18, 1920 Article [XIX] - Women's Suffrage Rights	78
Jan 23, 1933 Article [XX] - Terms of President, Vice President, Members of Congress: Presidential Vacancy	80
Mar 21, 1947 Article [XXI] - Repeal of Eighteenth Amendment	81
Feb 27, 1951 Amendment XXII - Presidential Tenure	81
Mar 29, 1961 Amendment XXIII - Presidential Electors for the District of Columbia	81
Jan 24, 1964 Amendment XXIV - Abolition of the Poll Tax Qualification in Federal Elections	81
Feb 10, 1967 Amendment XXV - Presidential Vacancy, Disability, and Inability	82
Jul 1, 1971 Amendment XXVI - Reduction of Voting Age Qualification	82
May 7, 1992 Amendment XXVII - Congressional Pay Limitation	82

THE UNITED STATES CONSTITUTION

Constitution Day is September 17.

We the People

(Preamble)

We the People of the United States, in Order to form a more perfect Union, establish Justice, insure domestic Tranquility, provide for the common defence, promote the general Welfare, and secure the Blessings of Liberty to ourselves and our Posterity, do ordain and establish this Constitution for the United States of America.

Article I
(Article 1 - Legislative)

Section 1

All legislative Powers herein granted shall be vested in a Congress of the United States, which shall consist of a Senate and House of Representatives.

THE CONSTITUTION OF THE UNITED STATES

Section 2

1: The House of Representatives shall be composed of Members chosen every second Year by the People of the several States, and the Electors in each State shall have the Qualifications requisite for Electors of the most numerous Branch of the State Legislature.

2: No Person shall be a Representative who shall not have attained to the Age of twenty five Years, and been seven Years a Citizen of the United States, and who shall not, when elected, be an Inhabitant of that State in which he shall be chosen.

3: Representatives and direct Taxes shall be apportioned among the several States which may be included within this Union, according to their respective Numbers, which shall be determined by adding to the whole Number of free Persons, including those bound to Service for a Term of Years, and excluding Indians not taxed, three fifths of all other Persons.[2] The actual Enumeration shall be made within three Years after the first Meeting of the Congress of the United States, and within every subsequent Term of ten Years, in such Manner as they shall by Law direct. The Number of Representatives shall not exceed one for every thirty Thousand, but each State shall have at Least one Representative; and until such enumeration shall be made, the State of New Hampshire shall be entitled to chuse three, Massachusetts eight, Rhode-Island and Providence Plantations one, Connecticut five, New-York six, New Jersey four, Pennsylvania eight, Delaware one, Maryland six, Virginia ten, North Carolina five, South Carolina five, and Georgia three.

4: When vacancies happen in the Representation from any State, the Executive Authority thereof shall issue Writs of Election to fill such Vacancies.

5: The House of Representatives shall chuse their Speaker and other Officers; and shall have the sole Power of Impeachment.

Section 3

1: The Senate of the United States shall be composed of two Senators from each State, chosen by the Legislature thereof,[3] for six Years; and each Senator shall have one Vote.

2: Immediately after they shall be assembled in Consequence of the first Election, they shall be divided as equally as may be into three Classes. The Seats of the Senators of the first Class shall be vacated at the Expiration of the second Year, of the second Class at the Expiration of the fourth Year, and of the third Class at the Expiration of the sixth Year, so that one third may be chosen every second Year; and if Vacancies happen by Resignation, or otherwise, during the Recess of the Legislature of any State, the Executive thereof may make temporary Appointments until the next Meeting of the Legislature, which shall then fill such Vacancies.[4]

3: No Person shall be a Senator who shall not have attained to the Age of thirty Years, and been nine Years a Citizen of the United States, and who shall not, when elected, be an Inhabitant of that State for which he shall be chosen.

4: The Vice President of the United States shall be President of the Senate, but shall have no Vote, unless they be equally divided.

5: The Senate shall chuse their other Officers, and also a President pro tempore, in the Absence of the Vice President, or when he shall exercise the Office of President of the United States.

6: The Senate shall have the sole Power to try all Impeachments. When sitting for that Purpose, they shall be on Oath or Affirmation. When the President of the United States is tried, the Chief Justice shall preside: And no Person shall be convicted without the Concurrence of two thirds of the Members present.

7: Judgment in Cases of impeachment shall not extend further than to removal from Office, and disqualification to hold and enjoy any Office of honor, Trust or Profit under the United States: but the Party convicted shall nevertheless be liable and subject to Indictment, Trial, Judgment and Punishment, according to Law.

Section 4

1: The Times, Places and Manner of holding Elections for Senators and Representatives, shall be prescribed in each State by the Legislature thereof; but the Congress may at any time by Law make or alter such Regulations, except as to the Places of chusing Senators.

2: The Congress shall assemble at least once in every Year, and such Meeting shall be on the first Monday in December,[5] unless they shall by Law appoint a different Day.

Section 5

1: Each House shall be the Judge of the Elections, Returns and Qualifications of its own Members, and a Majority of each shall constitute a Quorum to do Business; but a smaller Number may adjourn from day to day, and may be authorized to compel the Attendance of absent Members, in such Manner, and under such Penalties as each House may provide.

2: Each House may determine the Rules of its Proceedings, punish its Members for disorderly Behaviour, and, with the Concurrence of two thirds, expel a Member.

3: Each House shall keep a Journal of its Proceedings, and from time to time publish the same, excepting such Parts as may in their Judgment require Secrecy; and the Yeas and Nays of the Members of either House on any question shall, at the Desire of one fifth of those Present, be entered on the Journal.

4: Neither House, during the Session of Congress, shall, without the Consent of the other, adjourn for more than three days, nor to any other Place than that in which the two Houses shall be sitting.

Section 6

1: The Senators and Representatives shall receive a Compensation for their Services, to be ascertained by Law, and paid out of the Treasury of the United States.[6] They shall in all Cases, except Treason, Felony and Breach of the Peace, be privileged from Arrest during their Attendance at the Session of their respective Houses, and in going to and returning from the same; and for any Speech or Debate in either House, they shall not be questioned in any other Place.

2: No Senator or Representative shall, during the Time for which he was elected, be appointed to any civil Office under the Authority of the United States, which shall have been created, or the Emoluments whereof shall have been encreased during such time; and no Person holding any Office under the United States, shall be a Member of either House during his Continuance in Office.

THE CONSTITUTION OF THE UNITED STATES

Section 7

1: All Bills for raising Revenue shall originate in the House of Representatives; but the Senate may propose or concur with Amendments as on other Bills.

2: Every Bill which shall have passed the House of Representatives and the Senate, shall, before it become a Law, be presented to the President of the United States; If he approve he shall sign it, but if not he shall return it, with his Objections to that House in which it shall have originated, who shall enter the Objections at large on their Journal, and proceed to reconsider it. If after such Reconsideration two thirds of that House shall agree to pass the Bill, it shall be sent, together with the Objections, to the other House, by which it shall likewise be reconsidered, and if approved by two thirds of that House, it shall become a Law. But in all such Cases the Votes of both Houses shall be determined by yeas and Nays, and the Names of the Persons voting for and against the Bill shall be entered on the Journal of each House respectively. If any Bill shall not be returned by the President within ten Days (Sundays excepted) after it shall have been presented to him, the Same shall be a Law, in like Manner as if he had signed it, unless the Congress by their Adjournment prevent its Return, in which Case it shall not be a Law.

3: Every Order, Resolution, or Vote to which the Concurrence of the Senate and House of Representatives may be necessary (except on a question of Adjournment) shall be presented to the President of the United States; and before the Same shall take Effect, shall be approved by him, or being disapproved by him, shall be repassed by two thirds of the Senate and House of Representatives, according to the Rules and Limitations prescribed in the Case of a Bill.

THE CONSTITUTION OF THE UNITED STATES

Section 8

1: The Congress shall have Power To lay and collect Taxes, Duties, Imposts and Excises, to pay the Debts and provide for the common Defence and general Welfare of the United States; but all Duties, Imposts and Excises shall be uniform throughout the United States;

2: To borrow Money on the credit of the United States;

3: To regulate Commerce with foreign Nations, and among the several States, and with the Indian Tribes;

4: To establish an uniform Rule of Naturalization, and uniform Laws on the subject of Bankruptcies throughout the United States;

5: To coin Money, regulate the Value thereof, and of foreign Coin, and fix the Standard of Weights and Measures;

6: To provide for the Punishment of counterfeiting the Securities and current Coin of the United States;

7: To establish Post Offices and post Roads;

8: To promote the Progress of Science and useful Arts, by securing for limited Times to Authors and Inventors the exclusive Right to their respective Writings and Discoveries;

9: To constitute Tribunals inferior to the supreme Court;

10: To define and punish Piracies and Felonies committed on the high Seas, and Offences against the Law of Nations;

11: To declare War, grant Letters of Marque and Reprisal, and make Rules concerning Captures on Land and Water;

12: To raise and support Armies, but no Appropriation of Money to that Use shall be for a longer Term than two Years;

13: To provide and maintain a Navy;

14: To make Rules for the Government and Regulation of the land and naval Forces;

15: To provide for calling forth the Militia to execute the Laws of the Union, suppress Insurrections and repel Invasions;

16: To provide for organizing, arming, and disciplining, the Militia, and for governing such Part of them as may be employed in the Service of the United States, reserving to the States respectively, the Appointment of the Officers, and the Authority of training the Militia according to the discipline prescribed by Congress;

17: To exercise exclusive Legislation in all Cases whatsoever, over such District (not exceeding ten Miles square) as may, by Cession of particular States, and the Acceptance of Congress, become the Seat of the Government of the United States, and to exercise like Authority over all Places purchased by the Consent of the Legislature of the State in which the Same shall be, for the Erection of Forts, Magazines, Arsenals, dock-Yards, and other needful Buildings;—And

18: To make all Laws which shall be necessary and proper for carrying into Execution the foregoing Powers, and all other Powers vested by this Constitution in the Government of the United States, or in any Department or Officer thereof.

THE CONSTITUTION OF THE UNITED STATES

Section 9

1: The Migration or Importation of such Persons as any of the States now existing shall think proper to admit, shall not be prohibited by the Congress prior to the Year one thousand eight hundred and eight, but a Tax or duty may be imposed on such Importation, not exceeding ten dollars for each Person.

2: The Privilege of the Writ of Habeas Corpus shall not be suspended, unless when in Cases of Rebellion or Invasion the public Safety may require it.

3: No Bill of Attainder or ex post facto Law shall be passed.

4: No Capitation, or other direct, Tax shall be laid, unless in Proportion to the Census or Enumeration herein before directed to be taken.[7]

5: No Tax or Duty shall be laid on Articles exported from any State.

6: No Preference shall be given by any Regulation of Commerce or Revenue to the Ports of one State over those of another: nor shall Vessels bound to, or from, one State, be obliged to enter, clear, or pay Duties in another.

7: No Money shall be drawn from the Treasury, but in Consequence of Appropriations made by Law; and a regular Statement and Account of the Receipts and Expenditures of all public Money shall be published from time to time.

8: No Title of Nobility shall be granted by the United States: And no Person holding any Office of Profit or Trust under them, shall, without the Consent of the Congress, accept of any present, Emolument, Office, or Title, of any kind whatever, from any King, Prince, or foreign State.

Section 10

1: No State shall enter into any Treaty, Alliance, or Confederation; grant Letters of Marque and Reprisal; coin Money; emit Bills of Credit; make any Thing but gold and silver Coin a Tender in Payment of Debts; pass any Bill of Attainder, ex post facto Law, or Law impairing the Obligation of Contracts, or grant any Title of Nobility.

2: No State shall, without the Consent of the Congress, lay any Imposts or Duties on Imports or Exports, except what may be absolutely necessary for executing it's inspection Laws: and the net Produce of all Duties and Imposts, laid by any State on Imports or Exports, shall be for the Use of the Treasury of the United States; and all such Laws shall be subject to the Revision and Controul of the Congress.

3: No State shall, without the Consent of Congress, lay any Duty of Tonnage, keep Troops, or Ships of War in time of Peace, enter into any Agreement or Compact with another State, or with a foreign Power, or engage in War, unless actually invaded, or in such imminent Danger as will not admit of delay.

Article II
(Article 2 - Executive)

Section 1

1: The executive Power shall be vested in a President of the United States of America. He shall hold his Office during the Term of four Years, and, together with the Vice President, chosen for the same Term, be elected, as follows

2: Each State shall appoint, in such Manner as the Legislature thereof may direct, a Number of Electors, equal to the whole Number of Senators and Representatives to which the State may be entitled in the Congress: but no Senator or Representative, or Person holding an Office of Trust or Profit under the United States, shall be appointed an Elector.

3: The Electors shall meet in their respective States, and vote by Ballot for two Persons, of whom one at least shall not be an Inhabitant of the same State with themselves. And they shall make a List of all the Persons voted for, and of the Number of Votes for each; which List they shall sign and certify, and transmit sealed to the Seat of the Government of the United States, directed to the President of the Senate. The President of the Senate shall, in the Presence of the Senate and House of Representatives, open all the Certificates, and the Votes shall then be counted. The Person having the greatest Number of Votes shall be the President, if such Number be a Majority of the whole Number of Electors appointed; and if there be more than one who have such Majority, and have an equal Number of Votes, then the House of Representatives shall immediately chuse by Ballot one of them for President; and if no Person have a Majority, then from the five highest on the List the said House shall in like Manner chuse the President. But in chusing the President, the Votes shall be taken by States, the Representation from each State having one Vote; A quorum for this Purpose shall consist of a Member or Members from two thirds of the States, and a Majority of all the States shall be necessary to a Choice. In every Case, after the Choice of the President, the Person having the greatest Number of Votes of the Electors shall be the Vice President. But if there should remain two or more who have equal Votes, the Senate shall chuse from them by Ballot the Vice President.[8]

THE CONSTITUTION OF THE UNITED STATES

4: The Congress may determine the Time of chusing the Electors, and the Day on which they shall give their Votes; which Day shall be the same throughout the United States.

5: No Person except a natural born Citizen, or a Citizen of the United States, at the time of the Adoption of this Constitution, shall be eligible to the Office of President; neither shall any Person be eligible to that Office who shall not have attained to the Age of thirty five Years, and been fourteen Years a Resident within the United States.

6: In Case of the Removal of the President from Office, or of his Death, Resignation, or Inability to discharge the Powers and Duties of the said Office,[9] the Same shall devolve on the VicePresident, and the Congress may by Law provide for the Case of Removal, Death, Resignation or Inability, both of the President and Vice President, declaring what Officer shall then act as President, and such Officer shall act accordingly, until the Disability be removed, or a President shall be elected.

7: The President shall, at stated Times, receive for his Services, a Compensation, which shall neither be encreased nor diminished during the Period for which he shall have been elected, and he shall not receive within that Period any other Emolument from the United States, or any of them.

8: Before he enter on the Execution of his Office, he shall take the following Oath or Affirmation:—"I do solemnly swear (or affirm) that I will faithfully execute the Office of President of the United States, and will to the best of my Ability, preserve, protect and defend the Constitution of the United States."

Section 2

1: The President shall be Commander in Chief of the Army and Navy of the United States, and of the Militia of the several States, when called into the actual Service of the United States; he may require the Opinion, in writing, of the principal Officer in each of the executive Departments, upon any Subject relating to the Duties of their respective Offices, and he shall have Power to grant Reprieves and Pardons for Offences against the United States, except in Cases of Impeachment.

2: He shall have Power, by and with the Advice and Consent of the Senate, to make Treaties, provided two thirds of the Senators present concur; and he shall nominate, and by and with the Advice and Consent of the Senate, shall appoint Ambassadors, other public Ministers and Consuls, Judges of the supreme Court, and all other Officers of the United States, whose Appointments are not herein otherwise provided for, and which shall be established by Law: but the Congress may by Law vest the Appointment of such inferior Officers, as they think proper, in the President alone, in the Courts of Law, or in the Heads of Departments.

3: The President shall have Power to fill up all Vacancies that may happen during the Recess of the Senate, by granting Commissions which shall expire at the End of their next Session.

Section 3

He shall from time to time give to the Congress Information of the State of the Union, and recommend to their Consideration such Measures as he shall judge necessary and expedient; he may, on extraordinary Occasions, convene both Houses, or either of them, and in Case of Disagreement between them, with Respect to the Time of Adjournment, he may adjourn them to such Time as he shall think proper; he shall receive Ambassadors and other public Ministers; he shall take Care that the Laws be faithfully executed, and shall Commission all the Officers of the United States.

Section 4

The President, Vice President and all civil Officers of the United States, shall be removed from Office on Impeachment for, and Conviction of, Treason, Bribery, or other high Crimes and Misdemeanors.

Article III
(Article 3 - Judicial)

Section 1

The judicial Power of the United States, shall be vested in one supreme Court, and in such inferior Courts as the Congress may from time to time ordain and establish. The Judges, both of the supreme and inferior Courts, shall hold their Offices during good Behaviour, and shall, at stated Times, receive for their Services, a Compensation, which shall not be diminished during their Continuance in Office.

Section 2

1: The judicial Power shall extend to all Cases, in Law and Equity, arising under this Constitution, the Laws of the United States, and Treaties made, or which shall be made, under their Authority;—to all Cases affecting Ambassadors, other public Ministers and Consuls;—to all Cases of admiralty and maritime Jurisdiction;—to Controversies to which the United States shall be a Party;—to Controversies between two or more States;—between a State and Citizens of another State;*10* —between Citizens of different States, —between Citizens of the same State claiming

Lands under Grants of different States, and between a State, or the Citizens thereof, and foreign States, Citizens or Subjects.

2: In all Cases affecting Ambassadors, other public Ministers and Consuls, and those in which a State shall be Party, the supreme Court shall have original Jurisdiction. In all the other Cases before mentioned, the supreme Court shall have appellate Jurisdiction, both as to Law and Fact, with such Exceptions, and under such Regulations as the Congress shall make.

3: The Trial of all Crimes, except in Cases of Impeachment, shall be by Jury; and such Trial shall be held in the State where the said Crimes shall have been committed; but when not committed within any State, the Trial shall be at such Place or Places as the Congress may by Law have directed.

Section 3

1: Treason against the United States, shall consist only in levying War against them, or in adhering to their Enemies, giving them Aid and Comfort. No Person shall be convicted of Treason unless on the Testimony of two Witnesses to the same overt Act, or on Confession in open Court.

2: The Congress shall have Power to declare the Punishment of Treason, but no Attainder of Treason shall work Corruption of Blood, or Forfeiture except during the Life of the Person attainted.

Article IV
(Article 4 - States' Relations)

Section 1

Full Faith and Credit shall be given in each State to the public Acts, Records, and judicial Proceedings of every other State. And the Congress may by general Laws prescribe the Manner in which such Acts, Records and Proceedings shall be proved, and the Effect thereof.

Section 2

1: The Citizens of each State shall be entitled to all Privileges and Immunities of Citizens in the several States.

2: A Person charged in any State with Treason, Felony, or other Crime, who shall flee from Justice, and be found in another State, shall on Demand of the executive Authority of the State from which he fled, be delivered up, to be removed to the State having Jurisdiction of the Crime.

3: No Person held to Service or Labour in one State, under the Laws thereof, escaping into another, shall, in Consequence of any Law or Regulation therein, be discharged from such Service or Labour, but shall be delivered up on Claim of the Party to whom such Service or Labour may be due.*11*

Section 3

1: New States may be admitted by the Congress into this Union; but no new State shall be formed or erected within the Jurisdiction of any other State; nor any State be formed by the Junction of two or more States, or Parts of States, without the Consent of the Legislatures of the States concerned as well as of the Congress.

2: The Congress shall have Power to dispose of and make all needful Rules and Regulations respecting the Territory or other Property belonging to the United States; and nothing in this Constitution shall be so construed as to Prejudice any Claims of the United States, or of any particular State.

Section 4

The United States shall guarantee to every State in this Union a Republican Form of Government, and shall protect each of them against Invasion; and on Application of the Legislature, or of the Executive (when the Legislature cannot be convened) against domestic Violence.

Article V
(Article 5 - Mode of Amendment)

The Congress, whenever two thirds of both Houses shall deem it necessary, shall propose <u>Amendments</u> to this Constitution, or, on the Application of the Legislatures of two thirds of the several States, shall call a Convention for proposing Amendments, which, in either Case, shall be valid to all Intents and Purposes, as Part of this Constitution, when ratified by the Legislatures of three fourths of the several States, or by Conventions in three fourths thereof, as the one or the other Mode of Ratification may be proposed by the Congress; Provided that no Amendment which may be made prior to the Year One thousand eight hundred and eight shall in any Manner affect the first and fourth Clauses in the Ninth Section of the first Article; and that no State, without its Consent, shall be deprived of its equal Suffrage in the Senate.

Article VI
(Article 6 - Prior Debts, National Supremacy, Oaths of Offic)

1: All Debts contracted and Engagements entered into, before the Adoption of this Constitution, shall be as valid against the United States under this Constitution, as under the Confederation.

2: This Constitution, and the Laws of the United States which shall be made in Pursuance thereof; and all Treaties made, or which shall be made, under the Authority of the United States, shall be the supreme Law of the Land; and the Judges in every State shall be bound thereby, any Thing in the Constitution or Laws of any State to the Contrary notwithstanding.

3: The Senators and Representatives before mentioned, and the Members of the several State Legislatures, and all executive and judicial Officers, both of the United States and of the several States, shall be bound by Oath or Affirmation, to support this Constitution; but no religious Test shall ever be required as a Qualification to any Office or public Trust under the United States.

Article VII
(Article 7 - Ratification)

The Ratification of the Conventions of nine States, shall be sufficient for the Establishment of this Constitution between the States so ratifying the Same.

The Word "the", being interlined between the seventh and eight Lines of the first Page, The Word "Thirty" being partly written on an Erazure in the fifteenth Line of the first Page. The Words "is tried" being interlined between the thirty second and thirty third Lines of the first Page and the

THE CONSTITUTION OF THE UNITED STATES

Word "the" being interlined between the forty third and forty fourth Lines of the second Page.

> **done** in Convention by the Unanimous Consent of the States present the Seventeenth Day of September in the Year of our Lord one thousand seven hundred and Eighty seven and of the Independence of the United States of America the Twelfth **In witness** whereof We have hereunto subscribed our Names,

Attest
William
Jackson
Secretary   G⁰: Washington -Presid ᵗ. and deputy from Virginia

Delaware
    Geo: Read
    Gunning Bedford jun
    John Dickinson
    Richard Bassett
    Jaco: Broom

Maryland
    James M⁰Henry
    Dan of Sᵗ Thoˢ. Jenifer
    Danˡ Carroll.

Virginia
    John Blair—
    James Madison Jr.

North Carolina
    Wm Blount
    Rich^d. Dobbs Spaight.
    Hu Williamson

South Carolina
    J. Rutledge
    Charles Cotesworth Pinckney
    Charles Pinckney
    Pierce Butler.

Georgia
    William Few
    Abr Baldwin

New Hampshire
    John Langdon
    Nicholas Gilman

Massachusetts
    Nathaniel Gorham
    Rufus King

Connecticut
    W^m. Saml. Johnson
    Roger Sherman

New York
    Alexander Hamilton

New Jersey
    Wil. Livingston
    David Brearley.
    W^m. Paterson.
    Jona: Dayton

Pennsylvania
    B Franklin
    Thomas Mifflin
    Robt Morris
    Geo. Clymer
    Thos. FitzSimons
    Jared Ingersoll
    James Wilson.
    Gouv Morris

THE CONSTITUTION OF THE UNITED STATES

Letter of Transmittal

In Convention. Monday September 17th 1787.

Present

The States of

New Hampshire, Massachusetts, Connecticut, Mr. Hamilton from New York, New Jersey, Pennsylvania, Delaware, Maryland, Virginia, North Carolina, South Carolina and Georgia.

Resolved, That the preceeding Constitution be laid before the United States in Congress assembled, and that it is the Opinion of this Convention, that it should afterwards be submitted to a Convention of Delegates, chosen in each State by the People thereof, under the Recommendation of its Legislature, for their Assent and Ratification; and that each Convention assenting to, and ratifying the Same, should give Notice thereof to the United States in Congress assembled. Resolved, That it is the Opinion of this Convention, that as soon as the Conventions of nine States shall have ratified this Constitution, the United States in Congress assembled should fix a Day on which Electors should be appointed by the States which shall have ratified the same, and a Day on which the Electors should assemble to vote for the President, and the Time and Place for commencing Proceedings under this Constitution.

That after such Publication the Electors should be appointed, and the Senators and Representatives elected: That the Electors should meet on the Day fixed for the Election of the President, and should transmit their Votes certified, signed, sealed and directed, as the Constitution requires, to the Secretary of the United States in Congress assembled, that the Senators and Representatives should convene at the Time and Place assigned; that the Senators should appoint a President of the Senate, for the sole Purpose of receiving, opening and counting the Votes for President; and, that after he shall be chosen, the Congress, together with the President, should, without Delay, proceed to execute this Constitution.

By the unanimous Order of the Convention

W. Jackson
Secretary.   G^o: Washington -Presid^t.

Letter of Transmittal to the President of Congress

In Convention. Monday September 17th 1787.

SIR:

We have now the honor to submit to the consideration of the United States in Congress assembled, that Constitution which has appeared to us the most advisable.

The friends of our country have long seen and desired that the power of making war, peace, and treaties, that of levying money, and regulating commerce, and the correspondent executive and judicial authorities, should be fully and effectually vested in the General Government of the Union; but the impropriety of delegating such extensive trust to one body of men is evident: hence results the necessity of a different organization.

It is obviously impracticable in the Federal Government of these States to secure all rights of independent sovereignty to each, and yet provide for the interest and safety of all. Individuals entering into society must give up a share of liberty to preserve the rest. The magnitude of the sacrifice must depend as well on situation and circumstance, as on the object to be obtained. It is at all times difficult to draw with precision the line between those rights which must be surrendered, and those which may be preserved; and, on the present occasion, this difficulty was increased by a difference among the several States as to their situation, extent, habits, and particular interests.

In all our deliberations on this subject, we kept steadily in our view that which appears to us the greatest interest of every true American, the consolidation of our Union, in which is involved our prosperity, felicity, safety—perhaps our national existence. This important consideration, seriously and deeply impressed on our minds, led each State in the Convention to be less rigid on points of inferior magnitude than might have been otherwise expected; and thus, the Constitution which we now present is the result of a spirit of amity, and of that mutual deference and concession, which the peculiarity of our political situation rendered indispensable.

That it will meet the full and entire approbation of every State is not, perhaps, to be expected; but each will, doubtless, consider, that had her interest alone been consulted, the consequences might have been particularly disagreeable or injurious to others; that it is liable to as few exceptions as could reasonably have been expected, we hope and believe; that it may promote the lasting welfare of that Country so dear to us all, and secure her freedom and happiness, is our most ardent wish.

With great respect,
we have the honor to be,
SIR,
your excellency's most obedient and humble servants:
GEORGE WASHINGTON, *President.*
By the unanimous order of the convention.

His Excellency
the President of Congress.

THE CONSTITUTION OF THE UNITED STATES

Amendments to the Constitution

(The procedure for changing the United States Constitution is Article V - Mode of Amendment)

(The Preamble to The Bill of Rights)

Congress OF THE United States

begun and held at the City of New-York, on Wednesday the fourth of March, one thousand seven hundred and eighty nine.

THE Conventions of a number of the States, having at the time of their adopting the Constitution, expressed a desire, in order to prevent misconstruction or abuse of its powers, that further declaratory and restrictive clauses should be added: And as extending the ground of public confidence in the Government, will best ensure the beneficent ends of its institution.

RESOLVED by the Senate and House of Representatives of the United States of America, in Congress assembled, two thirds of both Houses concurring, that the following Articles be proposed to the Legislatures of the several States, as amendments to the Constitution of the United States, all, or any of which Articles, when ratified by three fourths of the said Legislatures, to be valid to all intents and purposes, as part of the said Constitution; viz.

ARTICLES in addition to, and Amendment of the Constitution of the United States of America, proposed by Congress, and ratified by the Legislatures of the several States, pursuant to the fifth Article of the original Constitution. [12]

(Articles I through X are known as the Bill of Rights) [ratified]

Article the first. .... After the first enumeration required by the first Article of the Constitution, there shall be one Representative for every thirty thousand, until the number shall amount to one hundred, after which, the proportion shall be so regulated by Congress, that there shall be not less than one hundred Representatives, nor less than one Representative for every forty thousand persons, until the number of Representatives shall amount to two hundred, after which the proportion shall be so regulated by Congress, that there shall not be less than two hundred Representatives, nor more than one Representative for every fifty thousand persons.

Article the second. .... No law, varying the compensation for the services of the Senators and Representatives, shall take effect, until an election of Representatives shall have intervened. [see Amendment XXVII]

Article [I]
(Amendment 1 - Freedom of expression and religion) [13]

Congress shall make no law respecting an establishment of religion, or prohibiting the free exercise thereof; or abridging the freedom of speech, or of the press; or the right of the people peaceably to assemble, and to petition the Government for a redress of grievances.

Article [II]
(Amendment 2 - Bearing Arms)

A well regulated Militia, being necessary to the security of a free State, the right of the people to keep and bear Arms, shall not be infringed.

Article [III]
(Amendment 3 - Quartering Soldiers)

No Soldier shall, in time of peace be quartered in any house, without the consent of the Owner, nor in time of war, but in a manner to be prescribed by law.

Article [IV]
(Amendment 4 - Search and Seizure)

The right of the people to be secure in their persons, houses, papers, and effects, against unreasonable searches and seizures, shall not be violated, and no Warrants shall issue, but upon probable cause, supported by Oath or affirmation, and particularly describing the place to be searched, and the persons or things to be seized.

Article [V]
(Amendment 5 - Rights of Persons)

No person shall be held to answer for a capital, or otherwise infamous crime, unless on a presentment or indictment of a Grand Jury, except in cases arising in the land or naval forces, or in the Militia, when in actual service in time of War or public danger; nor shall any person be subject for the same offence to be twice put in jeopardy of life or limb; nor shall be compelled in any criminal case to be a witness against himself, nor be deprived of life, liberty, or property, without due process of law; nor shall private property be taken for public use, without just compensation.

Article [VI]

(Amendment 6 - Rights of Accused in Criminal Prosecutions)

In all criminal prosecutions, the accused shall enjoy the right to a speedy and public trial, by an impartial jury of the State and district wherein the crime shall have been committed, which district shall have been previously ascertained by law, and to be informed of the nature and cause of the accusation; to be confronted with the witnesses against him; to have compulsory process for obtaining witnesses in his favor, and to have the Assistance of Counsel for his defence.

Article [VII]

(Amendment 7 - Civil Trials)

In Suits at common law, where the value in controversy shall exceed twenty dollars, the right of trial by jury shall be preserved, and no fact tried by a jury, shall be otherwise re-examined in any Court of the United States, than according to the rules of the common law.

Article [VIII]

(Amendment 8 - Further Guarantees in Criminal Cases)

Excessive bail shall not be required, nor excessive fines imposed, nor cruel and unusual punishments inflicted.

Article [IX]

(Amendment 9 - Unenumerated Rights)

The enumeration in the Constitution, of certain rights, shall not be construed to deny or disparage others retained by the people.

Article [X]

(Amendment 10 - Reserved Powers)

The powers not delegated to the United States by the Constitution, nor prohibited by it to the States, are reserved to the States respectively, or to the people.

Attest,	Frederick Augustus Muhlenberg Speaker of the House of Representatives.
John Beckley, Clerk of the House of Representatives.	John Adams, Vice-President of the United States, and President of the Senate.
Sam. A. Otis Secretary of the Senate.	

(end of the Bill of Rights)

[Article XI]

(Amendment 11 - Suits Against States)

The Judicial power of the United States shall not be construed to extend to any suit in law or equity, commenced or prosecuted against one of the United States by Citizens of another State, or by Citizens or Subjects of any Foreign State. *ratified #11 affects 10*

[Article XII]

(Amendment 12 - Election of President)

The Electors shall meet in their respective states, and vote by ballot for President and Vice-President, one of whom, at least, shall not be an inhabitant of the same state with themselves; they shall name in their ballots the person voted for as President, and in distinct ballots the person voted for as Vice-President, and they shall make distinct lists of all persons voted for as President, and of all persons voted for as Vice-President, and of the number of votes for each, which lists they shall sign and certify, and transmit sealed to the seat of the government of the

United States, directed to the President of the Senate;—The President of the Senate shall, in the presence of the Senate and House of Representatives, open all the certificates and the votes shall then be counted;—The person having the greatest number of votes for President, shall be the President, if such number be a majority of the whole number of Electors appointed; and if no person have such majority, then from the persons having the highest numbers not exceeding three on the list of those voted for as President, the House of Representatives shall choose immediately, by ballot, the President. But in choosing the President, the votes shall be taken by states, the representation from each state having one vote; a quorum for this purpose shall consist of a member or members from two-thirds of the states, and a majority of all the states shall be necessary to a choice. And if the House of Representatives shall not choose a President whenever the right of choice shall devolve upon them, before the fourth day of March next following, then the Vice-President shall act as President, as in the case of the death or other constitutional disability of the President.[14] —The person having the greatest number of votes as Vice-President, shall be the Vice-President, if such number be a majority of the whole number of Electors appointed, and if no person have a majority, then from the two highest numbers on the list, the Senate shall choose the Vice-President; a quorum for the purpose shall consist of two-thirds of the whole number of Senators, and a majority of the whole number shall be necessary to a choice. But no person constitutionally ineligible to the office of President shall be eligible to that of Vice-President of the United States. *ratified #12 affects 8*

THE CONSTITUTION OF THE UNITED STATES

Article XIII

(Amendment 13 - Slavery and Involuntary Servitude)

Neither slavery nor involuntary servitude, except as a punishment for crime whereof the party shall have been duly convicted, shall exist within the United States, or any place subject to their jurisdiction. *affects 11*

Congress shall have power to enforce this article by appropriate legislation. *ratified #13*

Article XIV

(Amendment 14 - Rights Guaranteed: Privileges and Immunities of Citizenship, Due Process, and Equal Protection)

1: All persons born or naturalized in the United States, and subject to the jurisdiction thereof, are citizens of the United States and of the State wherein they reside. No State shall make or enforce any law which shall abridge the privileges or immunities of citizens of the United States; nor shall any State deprive any person of life, liberty, or property, without due process of law; nor deny to any person within its jurisdiction the equal protection of the laws.

2: Representatives shall be apportioned among the several States according to their respective numbers, counting the whole number of persons in each State, excluding Indians not taxed. But when the right to vote at any election for the choice of electors for President and Vice President of the United States, Representatives in Congress, the Executive and Judicial officers of a State, or the members of the Legislature thereof, is denied to any of the male inhabitants of such State, being twenty-one years of age,[15] and citizens of the United States, or in any way abridged, except for participation in rebellion, or other crime, the basis of representation therein shall be reduced in the proportion which the number of such male citizens shall bear to the whole number of male citizens twenty-one years of age in such State. *affects 2*

3: No person shall be a Senator or Representative in Congress, or elector of President and Vice President, or hold any office, civil or military, under the United States, or under any State, who, having previously taken an oath, as a member of Congress, or as an officer of the United States, or as a member of any State legislature, or as an executive or judicial officer of any State, to support the Constitution of the United States, shall have engaged in insurrection or rebellion against the same, or given aid or comfort to the enemies thereof. But Congress may by a vote of two-thirds of each House, remove such disability.

4: The validity of the public debt of the United States, authorized by law, including debts incurred for payment of pensions and bounties for services in suppressing insurrection or rebellion, shall not be questioned. But neither the United States nor any State shall assume or pay any debt or obligation incurred in aid of insurrection or rebellion against the United States, or any claim for the loss or emancipation of any slave; but all such debts, obligations and claims shall be held illegal and void.

5: The Congress shall have power to enforce, by appropriate legislation, the provisions of this article. *ratified #14*

Article XV
(Amendment 15 - Rights of Citizens to Vote)

The right of citizens of the United States to vote shall not be denied or abridged by the United States or by any State on account of race, color, or previous condition of servitude.

The Congress shall have power to enforce this article by appropriate legislation. *ratified #15*

Article XVI
(Amendment 16 - Income Tax)

The Congress shall have power to lay and collect taxes on incomes, from whatever source derived, without apportionment among the several States, and without regard to any census or enumeration. *ratified #16 affects 2*

[Article XVII]
(Amendment 17 - Popular Election of Senators)

1: The Senate of the United States shall be composed of two Senators from each State, elected by the people thereof, for six years; and each Senator shall have one vote. The electors in each State shall have the qualifications requisite for electors of the most numerous branch of the State legislatures. *affects 3*

2: When vacancies happen in the representation of any State in the Senate, the executive authority of such State shall issue writs of election to fill such vacancies: Provided, That the legislature of any State may empower the executive thereof to make temporary appointments until the people fill the vacancies by election as the legislature may direct. *affects 4*

3: This amendment shall not be so construed as to affect the election or term of any Senator chosen before it becomes valid as part of the Constitution. *ratified #17*

Article [XVIII]
(Amendment 18 - Prohibition of Intoxicating Liquors)[16]

1: After one year from the ratification of this article the manufacture, sale, or transportation of intoxicating liquors within, the importation thereof into, or the exportation thereof from the United States and all territory subject to the jurisdiction thereof for beverage purposes is hereby prohibited.

2: The Congress and the several States shall have concurrent power to enforce this article by appropriate legislation.

3: This article shall be inoperative unless it shall have been ratified as an amendment to the Constitution by the legislatures of the several States, as provided in the Constitution, within seven years from the date of the submission hereof to the States by the Congress. *ratified #18*

Article [XIX]
(Amendment 19 - Women's Suffrage Rights)

The right of citizens of the United States to vote shall not be denied or abridged by the United States or by any State on account of sex. *affects 15*

Congress shall have power to enforce this article by appropriate legislation. *ratified #19*

Article [XX]
(Amendment 20 - Terms of President, Vice President, Members of Congress: Presidential Vacancy)

1: The terms of the President and Vice President shall end at noon on the 20th day of January, and the terms of Senators and Representatives at noon on the 3d day of January, of the years in which such terms would have ended if this article had not been ratified; and the terms of their successors shall then begin. *affects 5*

2: The Congress shall assemble at least once in every year, and such meeting shall begin at noon on the 3d day of January, unless they shall by law appoint a different day. *affects 5*

3: If, at the time fixed for the beginning of the term of the President, the President elect shall have died, the Vice President elect shall become President. If a President shall not have been chosen before the time fixed for the beginning of his term, or if the President elect shall have failed to qualify, then the Vice President elect shall act as President until a President shall have qualified; and the Congress may by law provide for the case wherein neither a President elect nor a Vice President elect shall have qualified, declaring who shall then act as President, or the manner in which one who is to act shall be selected, and such person shall act accordingly until a President or Vice President shall have qualified. *affects 9 affects 14*

4: The Congress may by law provide for the case of the death of any of the persons from whom the House of Representatives may choose a President whenever the right of choice shall have devolved upon them, and for the case of the death of any of the persons from whom the Senate may choose a Vice President whenever the right of choice shall have devolved upon them. *affects 9*

5: Sections 1 and 2 shall take effect on the 15th day of October following the ratification of this article.

6: This article shall be inoperative unless it shall have been ratified as an amendment to the Constitution by the legislatures of three-fourths of the several States within seven years from the date of its submission. *ratified #20*

Article [XXI]
(Amendment 21 - Repeal of Eighteenth Amendment)

1: The eighteenth article of amendment to the Constitution of the United States is hereby repealed. *affects 16*

2: The transportation or importation into any State, Territory, or possession of the United States for delivery or use therein of intoxicating liquors, in violation of the laws thereof, is hereby prohibited.

3: This article shall be inoperative unless it shall have been ratified as an amendment to the Constitution by conventions in the several States, as provided in the Constitution, within seven years from the date of the submission hereof to the States by the Congress. *ratified #21*

Amendment XXII
(Amendment 22 - Presidential Tenure)

1: No person shall be elected to the office of the President more than twice, and no person who has held the office of President, or acted as President, for more than two years of a term to which some other person was elected President shall be elected to the office of the President more than once. But this article shall not apply to any person holding the office of President when this article was proposed by the Congress, and shall not prevent any person who may be holding the office of President, or acting as President, during the term within which this article becomes operative from holding the office of President or acting as President during the remainder of such term.

2: This article shall be inoperative unless it shall have been ratified as an amendment to the Constitution by the legislatures of three-fourths of the several states within seven years from the date of its submission to the states by the Congress. *ratified #22*

Amendment XXIII

(Amendment 23 - Presidential Electors for the District of Columbia)

1: The District constituting the seat of government of the United States shall appoint in such manner as the Congress may direct: A number of electors of President and Vice President equal to the whole number of Senators and Representatives in Congress to which the District would be entitled if it were a state, but in no event more than the least populous state; they shall be in addition to those appointed by the states, but they shall be considered, for the purposes of the election of President and Vice President, to be electors appointed by a state; and they shall meet in the District and perform such duties as provided by the twelfth article of amendment.

2: The Congress shall have power to enforce this article by appropriate legislation. *ratified #23*

Amendment XXIV

(Amendment 24 - Abolition of the Poll Tax Qualification in Federal Elections)

1. The right of citizens of the United States to vote in any primary or other election for President or Vice President, for electors for President or Vice President, or for Senator or Representative in Congress, shall not be denied or abridged by the United States or any state by reason of failure to pay any poll tax or other tax.

2. The Congress shall have power to enforce this article by appropriate legislation. *ratified #24*

Amendment XXV *affects 9*

(Amendment 25 - Presidential Vacancy, Disability, and Inability)

1: In case of the removal of the President from office or of his death or resignation, the Vice President shall become President.

2: Whenever there is a vacancy in the office of the Vice President, the President shall nominate a Vice President who shall take office upon confirmation by a majority vote of both Houses of Congress.

3: Whenever the President transmits to the President pro tempore of the Senate and the Speaker of the House of Representatives his written declaration that he is unable to discharge the powers and duties of his office, and until he transmits to them a written declaration to the contrary, such powers and duties shall be discharged by the Vice President as Acting President.

4: Whenever the Vice President and a majority of either the principal officers of the executive departments or of such other body as Congress may by law provide, transmit to the President pro tempore of the Senate and the Speaker of the House of Representatives their written declaration that the President is unable to discharge the powers and duties of his office, the Vice President shall immediately assume the powers and duties of the office as Acting President.

Thereafter, when the President transmits to the President pro tempore of the Senate and the Speaker of the House of Representatives his written declaration that no inability exists, he shall resume the powers and duties of his office unless the Vice President and a majority of either the principal officers of the executive department or of such other body as Congress may by law provide, transmit within four days to the President pro tempore of the Senate and the Speaker of the House of Representatives their written declaration that the President is unable to discharge the powers and duties of his office. Thereupon Congress shall decide the issue, assembling within forty-eight hours for that purpose if not in session. If the Congress, within twenty-one days after receipt of the latter written declaration, or, if Congress is not in session, within twenty-one days after Congress is required to assemble, determines by two-thirds vote of both Houses that the President is unable to discharge the powers and duties of his office, the Vice President shall continue to discharge the same as Acting President; otherwise, the President shall resume the powers and duties of his office. *ratified #25*

Amendment XXVI

(Amendment 26 - Reduction of Voting Age Qualification)

1: The right of citizens of the United States, who are 18 years of age or older, to vote, shall not be denied or abridged by the United States or any state on account of age. *affects 15*

2: The Congress shall have the power to enforce this article by appropriate legislation. *ratified #26*

Amendment XXVII

(Amendment 27 - Congressional Pay Limitation)

No law varying the compensation for the services of the Senators and Representatives shall take effect until an election of Representatives shall have intervened. *ratified #27*

THE CONSTITUTION OF THE UNITED STATES

NOTES

Note 1: This text of the Constitution follows the engrossed copy signed by Gen. Washington and the deputies from 12 States. The arabic numerals preceding the paragraphs designate Clauses, and were not printed (but are referred to) in the original and have no reference to footnotes that appear as small superior figures (superscripts). *ratification*

Note 2: The part of Article 1 Section 2 Clause 3 relating to the mode of apportionment of representatives among the several States has been affected by Amendment XIV Section 2, and as to taxes on incomes without apportionment by Amendment XVI.

Note 3: Article 1 Section 3 Clause 1 has been affected by Amendment XVII Section 1.

Note 4: Article 1 Section 3 Clause 2 has been affected by Amendment XVII Section 2.

Note 5: Article 1 Section 4 Clause 2 has been affected by Amendment XX.

Note 6: Article 1 Section 6 Clause 1 has been affected by Amendment XXVII.

Note 7: Article 1 Section 9 Clause 4 has been affected by Amendment XVI.

Note 8: Article 2 Section 1 Clause 3 has been superseded by Amendment XII.

Note 9: Article 2 Section 1 Clause 6 has been affected by Amendment XX and Amendment XXV.

Note 10: Article 3 Section 2 Clause 1 has been affected by Amendment XI.

Note 11: Article 4 Section 2 Clause 3 has been affected by Amendment XIII Section 1.

Note 12: The first ten amendments to the Constitution of the United States are known as the Bill of Rights

Note 13: The Bill of Rights only had ten of the twelve articles ratified and these were then renumbered. Of the others only the 13th, 14th, 15th, and 16th articles of amendment had numbers assigned to them at the time of ratification.

Note 14: This sentence of Amendment XII has been superseded by Amendment XX Section 3.

Note 15: Article XIV Section 2 is modified by Amendment XIX Section 1 and Amendment XXVI Section 1.

Note 16: Amendment XVIII repealed by Amendment XXI Section 1.

Dates

- **May 25, 1787:** The Constitutional Convention opens with a quorum of seven states in Philadelphia to discuss revising the Articles of Confederation. Eventually all states but Rhode Island are represented.
- **Sept. 17, 1787:** All 12 state delegations approve the Constitution, 39 delegates sign it of the 42 present, and the Convention formally adjourns.
- **June 21, 1788:** The Constitution becomes effective for the ratifying states when New Hampshire is the ninth state to ratify it.
- **Mar. 4, 1789:** The first Congress under the Constitution convenes in New York City.
- **Apr. 30, 1789:** George Washington is inaugurated as the first President of the United States.
- **June 8, 1789:** James Madison introduces proposed Bill of Rights in the House of Representatives.
- **Sept. 24, 1789:** Congress establishes a Supreme Court, 13 district courts, three ad hoc circuit courts, and the position of Attorney General.
- **Sept. 25, 1789:** Congress approves 12 amendments and sends them to the states for ratification.
- **Feb. 2, 1790:** Supreme Court convenes for the first time after an unsuccessful attempt February 1.
- **Dec. 15, 1791:** Virginia ratifies the Bill of Rights, and 10 of the 12 proposed amendments become part of the U.S. Constitution.

THE CONSTITUTION OF THE UNITED STATES

Spellings

Some words now have different spellings:

behaviour
- behavior

chuse
- choose

chusing
- choosing

controul
- control

defence
- defense

encreased
- increased

erazure
- erasure

labour
- labor

offences
- offenses

Punctuation, hyphenation and grammar usage have also changed.

THE CONSTITUTION OF THE UNITED STATES

Vocabulary

3d
- 3rd (third)

abridged
- shortened

adjourn
- suspend proceedings to another time

adjournment
- suspending proceedings to another time

appellate
- appeal (review decision)

appropriation
- authorize spending

apportioned
- distributed

apportionment
- distributing

attainted
- disgrace

Bill of Attainder
- legislative act pronouncing guilt without trial

capitation
- poll tax

cession
- grant

comity
> - courteous recognition of laws and institutions of another (state)

commenced
> - started

concur
> - agree

concurrant
> - at the same time

concurrence
> - agreement

concurring
> - in agreement

construed
> - interpreted

Corruption of Blood
> - punishment of person and heirs

counsel
> - lawyer

declaratory
> - explaining law or right

democracy
> - this word is not in these documents directly, but "We the people" and "Republican Form of Government" are - most people say our form of government is a "Federal Democratic Republic"

devolved
> - passed on or delegated to another

disparage
- belittle
duties
- job
duties
- charge (like a tax)
duty
- job
duty
- charge (like a tax)
Duty of Tonnage
- charge by weight
emolument
- power and/or pay
emoluments
- power and/or pay
engrossed
- final draft
enumeration
- count or list
ex post facto
- *(latin)* after the fact
excises
- internal taxes
Habeas Corpus
- a writ in court for release of unlawful restraint - *(latin)* produce body [of evidence]

imminent
- about to occur - do not confuse with eminent or immanent

impeachment
- formal accusation of wrongdoing

impeachments
- formal accusations of wrongdoing

imposts
- taxes or duties, that are imposed

indictment
- formal charges

jurisdiction
- right to control

Letters of Marque
- (grant right of piracy) - document issued by a nation allowing a private citizen to seize citizens or goods of another nation

magazines
- ammunition storerooms

ordain
- order

prescribed
- establish a rule

privileged
- rights given a group

pro tempore
- temporary - *(latin)* for a time

posterity
- descendants

quartered
- housed

quartering
- housing

quorum
- minimum valid number of people

redress
- correct a wrong

repassed
- passed again

reprisal
- retaliation

republican
- representative and officers elected by citizens and responsible to them

suffrage
- vote
- voting

tranquility
- peace

treason
- betrayal of country

vessels
- ships

vested
- given the right

viz.

> - abbreviation for *(latin)* videlicet - namely (and when read aloud spoken as namely) *from: The Columbia Guide to Standard American English*

welfare

> - well-being

writ

> - order

writs

> - orders

How to read Roman numerals:

- The upper case letter I represents the arabic 1.
- The upper case letter V represents the arabic 5.
- The upper case letter X represents the arabic 10.
- The upper case letter L represents the arabic 50. (not used in this document)
- The upper case letter C represents the arabic 100. (not used in this document)
- The upper case letter D represents the arabic 500. (not used in this document)
- The upper case letter M represents the arabic 1,000. (not used in this document)
- A bar placed over a letter or group of letters multiplies that value by 1,000. (not used in this document)
- If the letter to the right represents an equal or smaller value the numbers ADD. XXII is 22.

THE CONSTITUTION OF THE UNITED STATES

- If the letter to the right is a larger value then the numbers SUBTRACT. IV is 4. Only I is used with V or X, X with L or C, and C with D or M.
- There is no zero!
- Both C and M often still appear in commerce mixed with arabic therefore if someone orders a quantity of 5M, they want 5,000 not 5 million.
- A few more samples: XCV = 95, XIII = 13, XCIX = 99, XLIX = 49

Given (first) name abbreviations:

George
- G^o:
- Geo:
- Geo.

Jacob
- Jaco:

Daniel
- Dan
- Danl

William
- W^m
- W^m.
- Wil.

Richard
- Rich^d

John
- J.

Abraham
- Abr
Samuel
- Saml
- Sam.
Johnathan
- Jona:
Robert
- Robt
Thomas
- Thos
Gouverneur
- Gouv

Of course B Franklin is Benjamin Franklin, jun and Jr. are junior, and Presid^t. is President.

Subject Index

A

- Admiralty and; maritime cases - Article III Section 2
- Advice and consent - Article II Section 2 Clause 2
- Age, as qualification for public office
    - President - Article II Section 1 Clause 5
    - Representatives - Article I Section 2 Clause 2
    - Senators - Article I Section 3 Clause 3
- Age, voting - Amendement XXVI
- Ambassadors
    - Case controversies - Article III Section 2 Clause 1
    - President's power - Article II Section 2 Clause 2; Article II Section 3
- Amendment procedure - Article V
- Appellate jurisdiction - Article III Section 2 Clause 2
- Appointment power - Article II Section 2 Clause 2
- Appointments, temporary - Amendement XVII Section 2
- Apportionment of representatives - Article I Section 2 Clause 3; Amendment XIV Section 2
- Appropriations(s) - Article I Section 8
- Arms, right to bear - Amendment II
- Army - Article II Section 2 Clause 1
- Assembly, right of - Amendement 1
- Authors - Article I Section 8 Clause 8

THE CONSTITUTION OF THE UNITED STATES

B

- Bail, excessive - <u>Amendement 8</u>
- Bankruptcy, Congress, power - <u>Article I Section 8 Clause 4</u>
- Bill of Rights (Amendments 1-10) - <u>Amendments I-X</u>
- Bills - <u>Article I Section 7</u>
- Bills of attainder - <u>Article I Section 9 Clause 3</u>; <u>Article I Section 10 Clause 1</u>
- Borrowing, Congress, power - <u>Article I Section 8 Clause 2</u>

C

- Cabinet officers, reports - <u>Article II Section 2 Clause 1</u>
- Census - <u>Article I Section 2 Clause 3</u>
- Chief Justice, role in impeachment trials - <u>Article I Section 3 Clause 6</u>
- Commander in Chief - <u>Article II Section 2 Clause 1</u>
- Commerce, Congress, power - <u>Article I Section 8 Clause 3</u>
- Commission of officers - <u>Article II Section 3 Clause 5</u>
- Compact - <u>Article I Section 10 Clause 3</u>
- Congress
  - annual meetings - <u>Article I Section 4 Clause 2</u>;
  - declaring war - <u>Article I Section 8 Clauses 11-14</u>
  - legislative proceedings - <u>Article I Section 5 Clause 2</u>
  - members, compensation and privileges - <u>Article I Section 6 Clause 1</u>;
  - organization - <u>Article I Section 1</u>
  - powers - <u>Article I Section 8</u>; <u>Amendement XII</u>
  - special sessions - <u>Article II Section 3</u>
- Congressional Record (Journal) - <u>Article I Section 5 Clause 3</u>

THE CONSTITUTION OF THE UNITED STATES

- Constitution, purpose - Preamble
- Contracts, interference by states - Article I Section 10 Clause 3
- Controversies, court cases - Article III Section 2 Clause 1
- Conventions - Article V;VII; Amendement 21 Section 3
- Copyrights & patents, Congress' power - Article I Section 8 Clause 8
- Counsel, right to - Amendement 6
- Counterfeiting, Congress' power to punish - Article I Section 8 Clause 6
- Courts - (see Judiciary)
- Criminal proceedings, rights of accused - Amendement 5; Amendement 6
- Currency, Congress' power - Article I Section 8 Clause 5

D

- Defense, Congress' power - Article I Section 8
- District of Columbia - Article I Section 8 Clause 17; Amendement XXIII Section 1
- Double jeopardy - Amendement V
- Due process of law - Amendement V; Amendement XIV Section 1

E

- Electoral College - Article II Section 1 Clause 4; Amendement XII; Amendement XXIII Section 1
- Equal protection of laws - Amendement 14 Section 1
- Equity - Article III Section 2 Clause 1; Amendement 11
- Ex post facto laws - Article I Section 9 Clause 3; Article I Section 10 Clause 1
- Extradition of fugitives by states - Article IV Section 2 Clause 2

F

- Fines, excessive - Amendement VIII
- Foreign affairs, President's power - Article II Section 2 Clause 2
- Foreign commerce, Congress' power - Article I Section 8 Clause 1
- Full faith and credit" clause - Article IV Section 1

G

- General welfare, Congress' power - Article I Section 8 Clause 1
- Grand jury indictments - Amendement V
- Grievances, redress of - Amendement I

H

- Habeas corpus - Article I Section 9 Clause 2
- House of Representatives
    - election to & eligibility for - Article I Section 2 Clause 2
    - members' terms of office - Article I Section 2 Clause 1; Article I Section 6 Clause 2
    - Speaker of - Article I Section 2 Clause 5; Amendement 24; Amendement 25
    - special powers
        - impeachment - Article I Section 2 Clause 5
        - Presidential elections - Article II Section 1 Clause 3; Amendement 12
        - revenue bills - Article I Section 7 Clause 1
        - states' representation in - Article I Section 2 Clause 1; Article I Section 2 Clause 3
    - vacancies - Article I Section 2 Clause 4

THE CONSTITUTION OF THE UNITED STATES

I

- Immunities (see Privileges and immunities)
- Impeachment
  - officials subject to - Article II Section 4
  - penalties - Article I Section 3 Clause 7
  - power of, lodged in House - Article I Section 2 Clause 5
  - reasons - Article II Section 4
  - trials, Senate - Article I Section 3 Clause 6
- Indians, commerce with, Congress' power - Article I Section 8 Clause 3
- Inhabitant (see Resident) - Article I Section 2 Clause 2; Article I Section 3 Clause 3
- International law, Congress' power - Article I Section 8 Clause 3
- Inventors - Article I Section 8 Clause 8

J

- Judiciary
  - inferior courts - Article I Section 8 Clause 9; Article III Section 1
  - judicial review - Article III Section 2 Clause 2
  - jurisdiction - Article III Section 2 Section 2
  - nomination & confirmation of judges - Article II Section 2 Clause 2
  - Supreme Court - Article III Section 1
  - terms of office & compensation - Article III Section 1
- Jury trials - Article III Section 2 Clause 3; Amendment VI; Amendment VII

THE CONSTITUTION OF THE UNITED STATES

L

- "Lame duck" amendment - Amendment XX
- Liquor - Amendment XVIII; Amendment XXI

M

- Marque and reprisal, letters of - Article I Section 8 Clause 11
- Men (see Persons)
- Militia (Military) - Amendment II; Amendment V
  - congressional powers - Article I Section 8 Clause 15
  - presidential powers - Article II Section 2 Clause 1
- Money - Article I Section 8 Clause 5-6

N

- National debt - Article VI Clause 1
- Native Americans (see Indians)
- Naturalization - Article I Section 8 Clause 4
- Navy - Article I Section 8 Clause 13-14; Article II Section 2 Clause 1
- "Necessary and proper" clause - Article I Section 8 Clause 18
- Nominate - Article II Section 2 Clause 2; Amendment XXV

O

- Oath of office, federal and state - Article II Section 1 Clause 8; Article VI
- Original jurisdiction - Article III Section 2 Clause 2

THE CONSTITUTION OF THE UNITED STATES

P

- (subject index still being added)
- Pardons and reprieves, President's power - Article II Section 2 Clause 1
- People, powers reserved to - Amendment X
- Persons - Amendment XIV
- Petition the government, right to - Amendment I
- "Pocket veto" - Article I Section 7 Clause 2
- Poll tax, prohibition - Amendment XXIV
- Post offices & roads, Congress' power - Article I Section 8 Clause 7
- Presidency, succession to - Article II Section 1; Amendement 20; Amendement 25
- President
    - disability - A25,3
    - election - Article II Section 1; Amendement 12; Amendement 22; Amendement 23
    - eligibility for office - Article II Section 1
    - legislation, role in - Article I Section 7
    - oath of office - Article II Section 1
    - powers & duties - Article IV Section 2
    - term of office & compensation - Article II Section 1
- Press, freedom of - A1
- Privileges and immunities (of citizens) - Article IV Section 2; Amendement 14 Section 1
- Prohibition - Amendement 18; Amendement 21
- Property, taking for public use - Amendement 5
- Punishments, cruel and unusual - Amendement 8

63

THE CONSTITUTION OF THE UNITED STATES

R

- Ratification of Constitution - Article V
- Religion, freedom of - Amendment I
- Religious oaths - Article VI
- Resident (see Inhabitant) - Article II Section 1 Clause 5

S

- Search and seizure - Amendement 4
- Seas, Congress' power - Article I Section 8
- Secrecy - Article I Section 5
- Self-incrimination - Amendment 5
- Senate
    - election to & eligibility for - Article I Section 3
    - equal representation of states - V
    - officers - Article I Section 3
    - President of - Article I Section 3;Amendement 12
    - President of, pro tempore - Article I Section 3;Amendement 25
    - special powers
        - impeachment trials - Article I Section 3
        - Presidential appointments - Article II Section 2
        - treaties - Article II Section 2
    - terms of office - Article I Section 3; Article I Section 6
    - vacancies - Amendement 17
- Slavery, prohibition - Amendement 13; A14,4
- Soldiers, quartering of - Amendement 3
- Speech, freedom of - A1
- Spending, Congress' power - Article I Section 8

THE CONSTITUTION OF THE UNITED STATES

- State of Union message - Article II Section 3
- States
- and federal elections - Article I Section 4
- formation & admission to Union - Article IV Section 3
- powers requiring consent of Congress - Article I Section 10
- powers reserved to - Amendement 10
- protection against invasion, violence - Article IV Section 4
- republican form of government guaranteed - Article IV Section 4
- suits against - Article III Section 2; Amendement 11
- Sundays - Article I Section 7
- Supreme law of the land (Constitution) - VI

T

- Taxing power
  - in general - Article I Section 7 Clause 1; Article I Section 8 Clause 1
  - direct taxes prohibited - Article I Section 9 Clause 4
  - income taxes permitted - Amendment XVI
- Territories - Article IV Section 3 Clause 2
- Titles of nobility - Article I Section 9 Clause 8
- Treason - Article III Section 3
- Treaty(ies) - Article I Section 10 Clause 1; Article II Section 2 Clause 2; Article III Section 2 Clause 1; Article VI Clause 2
- Trial - Article I Section 3 Clause 6-7; Article III Section 2 Clause 3; Amendment VI; Amendment VII

V

- Veto, President's power - Article I Section 7 Clause 2
- Vice-President
    - conditions for assuming Presidency - Article II Section 1 Clause 6; Amendement XX Section 3; Amendment XXV
    - declaring President disabled, role in - Amendement XX Section 4; Amendment XXV
    - succession to - Amendement XX Section 4; Amendment XXV
    - Senate, role in - Article I Section 3 Clause 4; Amendment XII
    - term of office - Article II Section 1 Clause 1
- Voting rights - Amendment XIV; Amendment XXIV
    - blacks, former slaves - Amendment XV
    - eighteen-years-old - Amendement XXVI Section 1
    - women - Amendement XIX Section 1

W

- War powers (see Congress, declaring war, powers; President, powers & duties; States, protection against invasion)
- Warrants - Amendement IV
- Weights and measures, standards of - Article I Section 8 Clause 5
- Women - (see Persons)

Ratifications

The Constitution

The Constitution was adopted by a convention of the States on September 17, 1787, and was subsequently ratified by the several States, on the following dates: Delaware, December 7, 1787; Pennsylvania, December 12, 1787; New Jersey, December 18, 1787; Georgia, January 2, 1788; Connecticut, January 9, 1788; Massachusetts, February 6, 1788; Maryland, April 28, 1788; South Carolina, May 23, 1788; New Hampshire, June 21, 1788.

Ratification was completed on June 21, 1788.

The Constitution was subsequently ratified by Virginia, June 25, 1788; New York, July 26, 1788; North Carolina, November 21, 1789; Rhode Island, May 29, 1790; and Vermont, January 10, 1791.

In May 1785, a committee of Congress made a report recommending an alteration in the Articles of Confederation, but no action was taken on it, and it was left to the State Legislatures to proceed in the matter. In January 1786, the Legislature of Virginia passed a resolution providing for the appointment of five commissioners, who, or any three of them, should meet such commissioners as might be appointed in the other States of the Union, at a time and place to be agreed upon, to take into consideration the trade of the United States; to consider how far a uniform system in their commercial regulations may be necessary to their common interest and their permanent harmony; and to report to the several States such an act, relative to this great object, as, when ratified by them, will enable the United States in Congress effectually to provide for the same. The Virginia commissioners, after some correspondence, fixed the first Monday in September as the time, and the city of Annapolis as the place for the meeting, but only four other States were represented, viz: Delaware, New York, New Jersey, and Pennsylvania; the commissioners appointed by Massachusetts, New Hampshire, North Carolina, and Rhode Island failed to attend. Under the circumstances of so partial a representation, the commissioners present agreed upon a report, (drawn by Mr. Hamilton, of New York,) expressing their unanimous conviction that it might essentially tend to advance the interests of the Union if the States by which they were respectively delegated would concur, and use their endeavors to procure the concurrence of the other States, in the appointment of commissioners to meet at Philadelphia on the Second Monday of May following, to take into consideration the situation of the United States; to devise such further provisions as should appear to them necessary to render the Constitution of the Federal Government adequate to the exigencies of the Union; and to report such an act for that purpose to the United States in Congress assembled as, when agreed to by them and afterwards confirmed by the Legislatures of every State, would effectually provide for the same.

Congress, on the 21st of February, 1787, adopted a resolution in favor of a convention, and the Legislatures of those States which had not already done so (with the exception of Rhode Island) promptly appointed delegates. On the 25th of May, seven States having convened, George Washington, of Virginia, was unanimously elected President, and the consideration of the proposed constitution was commenced. On the 17th of September, 1787, the Constitution as engrossed and agreed upon was signed by all the members present, except Mr. Gerry of Massachusetts, and Messrs. Mason and Randolph, of Virginia. The president of the convention transmitted it to Congress, with a resolution stating how the proposed Federal Government should be put in operation, and an explanatory letter. Congress, on the 28th of September, 1787, directed the Constitution so framed, with the resolutions and letter concerning the same, to "be transmitted to the several Legislatures in order to be submitted to a convention of delegates chosen in each State by the people thereof, in conformity to the resolves of the convention."

On the 4th of March, 1789, the day which had been fixed for commencing the operations of Government under the new Constitution, it had been ratified by the conventions chosen in each State to consider it, as follows: Delaware, December 7, 1787; Pennsylvania, December 12, 1787; New Jersey, December 18, 1787; Georgia, January 2, 1788; Connecticut, January 9, 1788; Massachusetts, February 6, 1788; Maryland, April 28, 1788; South Carolina, May 23, 1788; New Hampshire, June 21, 1788; Virginia, June 25, 1788; and New York, July 26, 1788.

The President informed Congress, on the 28th of January, 1790, that North Carolina had ratified the Constitution November 21, 1789; and he informed Congress on the 1st of June, 1790, that Rhode Island had ratified the Constitution May 29, 1790. Vermont, in convention, ratified the Constitution January 10, 1791, and was, by an act of Congress approved February 18, 1791, "received and admitted into this Union as a new and entire member of the United States". *Constitution*

THE CONSTITUTION OF THE UNITED STATES

[Article I] through [Article X]
(The Bill of Rights)

The first ten amendments to the Constitution of the United States (and two others, one of which failed of ratification and the other which later became the 27th amendment) were proposed to the legislatures of the several States by the First Congress on September 25, 1789. The first ten amendments were ratified by the following States, and the notifications of ratification by the Governors thereof were successively communicated by the President to Congress: New Jersey, November 20, 1789; Maryland, December 19, 1789; North Carolina, December 22, 1789; South Carolina, January 19, 1790; New Hampshire, January 25, 1790; Delaware, January 28, 1790; New York, February 24, 1790; Pennsylvania, March 10, 1790; Rhode Island, June 7, 1790; Vermont, November 3, 1791; and Virginia, December 15, 1791.

Ratification was completed on December 15, 1791.

The amendments were subsequently ratified by the legislatures of Massachusetts, March 2, 1939; Georgia, March 18, 1939; and Connecticut, April 19, 1939. *Bill of Rights*

[Article XI]

The eleventh amendment to the Constitution of the United States was proposed to the legislatures of the several States by the Third Congress, on the 4th of March 1794; and was declared in a message from the President to Congress, dated the 8th of January, 1798, to have been ratified by the legislatures of three-fourths of the States. The dates of ratification were: NewYork, March 27, 1794; Rhode Island, March 31, 1794; Connecticut, May 8, 1794; New Hampshire, June 16, 1794;

Massachusetts, June 26, 1794; Vermont, between October 9, 1794 and November 9, 1794; Virginia, November 18, 1794; Georgia, November 29, 1794; Kentucky, December 7, 1794; Maryland, December 26, 1794; Delaware, January 23, 1795; North Carolina, February 7, 1795.

Ratification was completed on February 7, 1795.

The amendment was subsequently ratified by South Carolina on December 4, 1797. New Jersey and Pennsylvania did not take action on the amendment. *amendment 11*

[Article XII]

The twelfth amendment to the Constitution of the United States was proposed to the legislatures of the several States by the Eighth Congress, on the 9th of December, 1803, in lieu of the original third paragraph of the first section of the second article; and was declared in a proclamation of the Secretary of State, dated the 25th of September, 1804, to have been ratified by the legislatures of 13 of the 17 States. The dates of ratification were: North Carolina, December 21, 1803; Maryland, December 24, 1803; Kentucky, December 27, 1803; Ohio, December 30, 1803; Pennsylvania, January 5, 1804; Vermont, January 30, 1804; Virginia, February 3, 1804; New York, February 10, 1804; New Jersey, February 22, 1804; Rhode Island, March 12, 1804; South Carolina, May 15, 1804; Georgia, May 19, 1804; New Hampshire, June 15, 1804.

Ratification was completed on June 15, 1804.

The amendment was subsequently ratified by Tennessee, July 27, 1804.

The amendment was rejected by Delaware, January 18, 1804; Massachusetts, February 3, 1804; Connecticut, at its session begun May 10, 1804. *amendment 12*

Article XIII

The thirteenth amendment to the Constitution of the United States was proposed to the legislatures of the several States by the Thirty-eighth Congress, on the 31st day of January, 1865, and was declared, in a proclamation of the Secretary of State, dated the 18th of December, 1865, to have been ratified by the legislatures of twenty-seven of the thirty-six States. The dates of ratification were: Illinois, February 1, 1865; Rhode Island, February 2, 1865; Michigan, February 2, 1865; Maryland, February 3, 1865; New York, February 3, 1865; Pennsylvania, February 3, 1865; West Virginia, February 3, 1865; Missouri, February 6, 1865; Maine, February 7, 1865; Kansas, February 7, 1865; Massachusetts, February 7, 1865; Virginia, February 9, 1865; Ohio, February 10, 1865; Indiana, February 13, 1865; Nevada, February 16, 1865; Louisiana, February 17, 1865; Minnesota, February 23, 1865; Wisconsin, February 24, 1865; Vermont, March 9, 1865; Tennessee, April 7, 1865; Arkansas, April 14, 1865; Connecticut, May 4, 1865; New Hampshire, July 1, 1865; South Carolina, November 13, 1865; Alabama, December 2, 1865; North Carolina, December 4, 1865; Georgia, December 6, 1865.

Ratification was completed on December 6, 1865.

The amendment was subsequently ratified by Oregon, December 8, 1865; California, December 19, 1865; Florida, December 28, 1865 (Florida again ratified on June 9, 1868, upon its adoption of a new constitution); Iowa, January 15, 1866; New Jersey, January 23, 1866 (after having rejected the amendment on March 16, 1865); Texas, February 18, 1870;

Delaware, February 12, 1901 (after having rejected the amendment on February 8, 1865); Kentucky, March 18, 1976 (after having rejected it on February 24, 1865).

The amendment was rejected (and not subsequently ratified) by Mississippi, December 4, 1865. *amendment 13*

Article XIV

The fourteenth amendment to the Constitution of the United States was proposed to the legislatures of the several States by the Thirty-ninth Congress, on the 13th of June, 1866. It was declared, in a certificate of the Secretary of State dated July 28, 1868 to have been ratified by the legislatures of 28 of the 37 States. The dates of ratification were: Connecticut, June 25, 1866; New Hampshire, July 6, 1866; Tennessee, July 19, 1866; New Jersey, September 11, 1866 (subsequently the legislature rescinded its ratification, and on March 24, 1868, readopted its resolution of rescission over the Governor's veto, and on Nov. 12, 1980, expressed support for the amendment); Oregon, September 19, 1866 (and rescinded its ratification on October 15, 1868); Vermont, October 30, 1866; Ohio, January 4, 1867 (and rescinded its ratification on January 15, 1868); New York, January 10, 1867; Kansas, January 11, 1867; Illinois, January 15, 1867; West Virginia, January 16, 1867; Michigan, January 16, 1867; Minnesota, January 16, 1867; Maine, January 19, 1867; Nevada, January 22, 1867; Indiana, January 23, 1867; Missouri, January 25, 1867; Rhode Island, February 7, 1867; Wisconsin, February 7, 1867; Pennsylvania, February 12, 1867; Massachusetts, March 20, 1867; Nebraska, June 15, 1867; Iowa, March 16, 1868; Arkansas, April 6, 1868; Florida, June 9, 1868; North Carolina, July 4, 1868 (after having rejected it on December 14, 1866); Louisiana, July 9, 1868 (after having rejected it on February 6, 1867); South Carolina, July 9, 1868 (after having rejected it on December 20, 1866).

Ratification was completed on July 9, 1868.

The amendment was subsequently ratified by Alabama, July 13, 1868; Georgia, July 21, 1868 (after having rejected it on November 9, 1866); Virginia, October 8, 1869 (after having rejected it on January 9, 1867); Mississippi, January 17, 1870; Texas, February 18, 1870 (after having rejected it on October 27, 1866); Delaware, February 12, 1901 (after having rejected it on February 8, 1867); Maryland, April 4, 1959 (after having rejected it on March 23, 1867); California, May 6, 1959; Kentucky, March 18, 1976 (after having rejected it on January 8, 1867). *amendment 14*

Article XV

The fifteenth amendment to the Constitution of the United States was proposed to the legislatures of the several States by the Fortieth Congress, on the 26th of February, 1869, and was declared, in a proclamation of the Secretary of State, dated March 30, 1870, to have been ratified by the legislatures of twenty-nine of the thirty-seven States. The dates of ratification were: Nevada, March 1, 1869; West Virginia, March 3, 1869; Illinois, March 5, 1869; Louisiana, March 5, 1869; North Carolina, March 5, 1869; Michigan, March 8, 1869; Wisconsin, March 9, 1869; Maine, March 11, 1869; Massachusetts, March 12, 1869; Arkansas, March 15, 1869; South Carolina, March 15, 1869; Pennsylvania, March 25, 1869; New York, April 14, 1869 (and the legislature of the same State passed a resolution January 5, 1870, to withdraw its consent to it, which action it rescinded on March 30, 1970); Indiana, May 14, 1869; Connecticut, May 19, 1869; Florida, June 14, 1869; New Hampshire, July 1, 1869; Virginia, October 8, 1869; Vermont, October 20, 1869; Missouri, January 7, 1870;

THE CONSTITUTION OF THE UNITED STATES

Minnesota, January 13, 1870; Mississippi, January 17, 1870; Rhode Island, January 18, 1870; Kansas, January 19, 1870; Ohio, January 27, 1870 (after having rejected it on April 30, 1869); Georgia, February 2, 1870; Iowa, February 3, 1870.

Ratification was completed on February 3, 1870, unless the withdrawal of ratification by New York was effective; in which event ratification was completed on February 17, 1870, when Nebraska ratified.

The amendment was subsequently ratified by Texas, February 18, 1870; New Jersey, February 15, 1871 (after having rejected it on February 7, 1870); Delaware, February 12, 1901 (after having rejected it on March 18, 1869); Oregon, February 24, 1959; California, April 3, 1962 (after having rejected it on January 28, 1870); Kentucky, March 18, 1976 (after having rejected it on March 12, 1869).

The amendment was approved by the Governor of Maryland, May 7, 1973; Maryland having previously rejected it on February 26, 1870.

The amendment was rejected (and not subsequently ratified) by Tennessee, November 16, 1869. *amendment 15*

Article XVI

The sixteenth amendment to the Constitution of the United States was proposed to the legislatures of the several States by the Sixty-first Congress on the 12th of July, 1909, and was declared, in a proclamation of the Secretary of State, dated the 25th of February, 1913, to have been ratified by 36 of the 48 States. The dates of ratification were: Alabama, August 10, 1909; Kentucky, February 8, 1910; South Carolina, February 19, 1910; Illinois, March 1, 1910; Mississippi, March 7, 1910; Oklahoma, March 10, 1910; Maryland, April 8, 1910; Georgia, August 3, 1910; Texas,

August 16, 1910; Ohio, January 19, 1911; Idaho, January 20, 1911; Oregon, January 23, 1911; Washington, January 26, 1911; Montana, January 30, 1911; Indiana, January 30, 1911; California, January 31, 1911; Nevada, January 31, 1911; South Dakota, February 3, 1911; Nebraska, February 9, 1911; North Carolina, February 11, 1911; Colorado, February 15, 1911; North Dakota, February 17, 1911; Kansas, February 18, 1911; Michigan, February 23, 1911; Iowa, February 24, 1911; Missouri, March 16, 1911; Maine, March 31, 1911; Tennessee, April 7, 1911; Arkansas, April 22, 1911 (after having rejected it earlier); Wisconsin, May 26, 1911; New York, July 12, 1911; Arizona, April 6, 1912; Minnesota, June 11, 1912; Louisiana, June 28, 1912; West Virginia, January 31, 1913; New Mexico, February 3, 1913.

Ratification was completed on February 3, 1913.

The amendment was subsequently ratified by Massachusetts, March 4, 1913; New Hampshire, March 7, 1913 (after having rejected it on March 2, 1911).

The amendment was rejected (and not subsequently ratified) by Connecticut, Rhode Island, and Utah. *amendment 16*

[Article XVII]

The seventeenth amendment to the Constitution of the United States was proposed to the legislatures of the several States by the Sixty-second Congress on the 13th of May, 1912, and was declared, in a proclamation of the Secretary of State, dated the 31st of May, 1913, to have been ratified by the legislatures of 36 of the 48 States. The dates of ratification were: Massachusetts, May 22, 1912; Arizona, June 3, 1912; Minnesota, June 10, 1912; New York, January 15, 1913; Kansas, January 17, 1913;

Oregon, January 23, 1913; North Carolina, January 25, 1913; California, January 28, 1913; Michigan, January 28, 1913; Iowa, January 30, 1913; Montana, January 30, 1913; Idaho, January 31, 1913; West Virginia, February 4, 1913; Colorado, February 5, 1913; Nevada, February 6, 1913; Texas, February 7, 1913; Washington, February 7, 1913; Wyoming, February 8, 1913; Arkansas, February 11, 1913; Maine, February 11, 1913; Illinois, February 13, 1913; North Dakota, February 14, 1913; Wisconsin, February 18, 1913; Indiana, February 19, 1913; New Hampshire, February 19, 1913; Vermont, February 19, 1913; South Dakota, February 19, 1913; Oklahoma, February 24, 1913; Ohio, February 25, 1913; Missouri, March 7, 1913; New Mexico, March 13, 1913; Nebraska, March 14, 1913; New Jersey, March 17, 1913; Tennessee, April 1, 1913; Pennsylvania, April 2, 1913; Connecticut, April 8, 1913.

Ratification was completed on April 8, 1913.

The amendment was subsequently ratified by Louisiana, June 11, 1914.

The amendment was rejected by Utah (and not subsequently ratified) on February 26, 1913. *amendment 17*

Article [XVIII] [16]

The eighteenth amendment to the Constitution of the United States was proposed to the legislatures of the several States by the Sixty-fifth Congress, on the 18th of December, 1917, and was declared, in a proclamation of the Secretary of State, dated the 29th of January, 1919, to have been ratified by the legislatures of 36 of the 48 States. The dates of ratification were: Mississippi, January 8, 1918; Virginia, January 11, 1918; Kentucky, January 14, 1918; North Dakota, January 25, 1918; South Carolina, January 29, 1918; Maryland, February 13, 1918; Montana,

February 19, 1918; Texas, March 4, 1918; Delaware, March 18, 1918; South Dakota, March 20, 1918; Massachusetts, April 2, 1918; Arizona, May 24, 1918; Georgia, June 26, 1918; Louisiana, August 3, 1918; Florida, December 3, 1918; Michigan, January 2, 1919; Ohio, January 7, 1919; Oklahoma, January 7, 1919; Idaho, January 8, 1919; Maine, January 8, 1919; West Virginia, January 9, 1919; California, January 13, 1919; Tennessee, January 13, 1919; Washington, January 13, 1919; Arkansas, January 14, 1919; Kansas, January 14, 1919; Alabama, January 15, 1919; Colorado, January 15, 1919; Iowa, January 15, 1919; New Hampshire, January 15, 1919; Oregon, January 15, 1919; Nebraska, January 16, 1919; North Carolina, January 16, 1919; Utah, January 16, 1919; Missouri, January 16, 1919; Wyoming, January 16, 1919.

Ratification was completed on January 16, 1919. See Dillon v. Gloss, 256 U.S. 368, 376 (1921).

The amendment was subsequently ratified by Minnesota on January 17, 1919; Wisconsin, January 17, 1919; New Mexico, January 20, 1919; Nevada, January 21, 1919; New York, January 29, 1919; Vermont, January 29, 1919; Pennsylvania, February 25, 1919; Connecticut, May 6, 1919; and New Jersey, March 9, 1922.

The amendment was rejected (and not subsequently ratified) by Rhode Island. *amendment 18*

Women's Suffrage Rights Article [XIX]

The nineteenth amendment to the Constitution of the United States was proposed to the legislatures of the several States by the Sixty-sixth Congress, on the 4th of June, 1919, and was declared, in a proclamation of the Secretary of State, dated the 26th of August, 1920, to have been ratified by the legislatures of 36 of the 48 States. The dates of ratification were: Illinois, June 10, 1919 (and that State readopted its resolution of ratification June 17, 1919); Michigan, June 10, 1919; Wisconsin, June 10, 1919; Kansas, June 16, 1919; New York, June 16, 1919; Ohio, June 16, 1919; Pennsylvania, June 24, 1919; Massachusetts, June 25, 1919; Texas, June 28, 1919; Iowa, July 2, 1919; Missouri, July 3, 1919; Arkansas, July 28, 1919; Montana, August 2, 1919; Nebraska, August 2, 1919; Minnesota, September 8, 1919; New Hampshire, September 10, 1919; Utah, October 2, 1919; California, November 1, 1919; Maine, November 5, 1919; North Dakota, December 1, 1919; South Dakota, December 4, 1919; Colorado, December 15, 1919; Kentucky, January 6, 1920; Rhode Island, January 6, 1920; Oregon, January 13, 1920; Indiana, January 16, 1920; Wyoming, January 27, 1920; Nevada, February 7, 1920; New Jersey, February 9, 1920; Idaho, February 11, 1920; Arizona, February 12, 1920; New Mexico, February 21, 1920; Oklahoma, February 28, 1920; West Virginia, March 10, 1920; Washington, March 22, 1920; Tennessee, August 18, 1920.

Ratification was completed on August 18, 1920.

The amendment was subsequently ratified by Connecticut on September 14, 1920 (and that State reaffirmed on September 21, 1920); Vermont, February 8, 1921; Delaware, March 6, 1923 (after having rejected it on June 2, 1920); Maryland, March 29, 1941 (after having rejected it on February 24, 1920, ratification certified on February 25, 1958); Virginia, February 21, 1952 (after having rejected it on February 12, 1920); Alabama, September 8, 1953 (after having rejected it on September 22, 1919); Florida, May 13, 1969; South Carolina, July 1, 1969 (after having rejected it on January 28, 1920, ratification certified on August 22, 1973);

Georgia, February 20, 1970 (after having rejected it on July 24, 1919); Louisiana, June 11, 1970 (after having rejected it on July 1, 1920); North Carolina, May 6, 1971; Mississippi, March 22, 1984 (after having rejected it on March 29, 1920). *amendment 19*

Article [XX]

The twentieth amendment to the Constitution was proposed to the legislatures of the several states by the Seventy-Second Congress, on the 2d day of March, 1932, and was declared, in a proclamation by the Secretary of State, dated on the 6th day of February, 1933, to have been ratified by the legislatures of 36 of the 48 States. The dates of ratification were: Virginia, March 4, 1932; New York, March 11, 1932; Mississippi, March 16, 1932; Arkansas, March 17, 1932; Kentucky, March 17, 1932; New Jersey, March 21, 1932; South Carolina, March 25, 1932; Michigan, March 31, 1932; Maine, April 1, 1932; Rhode Island, April 14, 1932; Illinois, April 21, 1932; Louisiana, June 22, 1932; West Virginia, July 30, 1932; Pennsylvania, August 11, 1932; Indiana, August 15, 1932; Texas, September 7, 1932; Alabama, September 13, 1932; California, January 4, 1933; North Carolina, January 5, 1933; North Dakota, January 9, 1933; Minnesota, January 12, 1933; Arizona, January 13, 1933; Montana, January 13, 1933; Nebraska, January 13, 1933; Oklahoma, January 13, 1933; Kansas, January 16, 1933; Oregon, January 16, 1933; Delaware, January 19, 1933; Washington, January 19, 1933; Wyoming, January 19, 1933; Iowa, January 20, 1933; South Dakota, January 20, 1933; Tennessee, January 20, 1933; Idaho, January 21, 1933; New Mexico, January 21, 1933; Georgia, January 23, 1933; Missouri, January 23, 1933; Ohio, January 23, 1933; Utah, January 23, 1933.

Ratification was completed on January 23, 1933.

The amendment was subsequently ratified by Massachusetts on January 24, 1933; Wisconsin, January 24, 1933; Colorado, January 24, 1933; Nevada, January 26, 1933; Connecticut, January 27, 1933; New Hampshire, January 31, 1933; Vermont, February 2, 1933; Maryland, March 24, 1933; Florida, April 26, 1933. *amendment 20*

Article [XXI]

The twenty-first amendment to the Constitution was proposed to the several states by the Seventy-Second Congress, on the 20th day of February, 1933, and was declared, in a proclamation by the Secretary of State, dated on the 5th day of December, 1933, to have been ratified by 36 of the 48 States. The dates of ratification were: Michigan, April 10, 1933; Wisconsin, April 25, 1933; Rhode Island, May 8, 1933; Wyoming, May 25, 1933; New Jersey, June 1, 1933; Delaware, June 24, 1933; Indiana, June 26, 1933; Massachusetts, June 26, 1933; New York, June 27, 1933; Illinois, July 10, 1933; Iowa, July *amendment 21*

Amendment XXII

Passed by Congress March 21, 1947. Ratified February 27, 1951. *amendment 22*

Amendment XXIII

Passed by Congress June 16, 1960. Ratified March 29, 1961. *amendment 23*

Amendment XXIV

Passed by Congress August 27, 1962. Ratified January 23, 1964. *amendment 24*

Amendment XXV

Passed by Congress July 6, 1965. Ratified February 10, 1967. *amendment 25*

Amendment XXVI

Passed by Congress March 23, 1971. Ratified July 1, 1971. *amendment 26*

Amendment XXVII

Originally proposed Sept. 25, 1789. Ratified May 7, 1992.

The date of September 25, 1789, is correct. The amendment was initially ratified by 6 states (MD, NC, SC, DE, VT, VA), and the other 8 states excluded, omitted, rejected, or excepted it. The amendment was ratified by various states over time, and in 1992 was fully ratified as an amendment to the Constitution.

For more information see: United States. The Constitution of the United States of America : with a summary of the actions by the states in ratification thereof ; to which is appended, for its historical interest, the Constitution of the Confederate States of America / prepared and distributed by the Virginia on Constitutional Government. Richmond : Virginia Commission on Constitutional Government, 1961. 94 p.

amendment 27